Smarty Marty

STEPS UP HER

GAME

Smarty Marty
STEPS UP HER
GAME

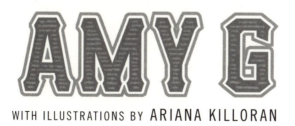

AMY G

WITH ILLUSTRATIONS BY ARIANA KILLORAN

cameron kids

Text copyright © 2017 by Amy Gutierrez
Illustrations copyright © 2017 by Cameron + Company

Book design by Melissa Nelson Greenberg

Library of Congress Cataloging-in-Publication Data available.
ISBN: 978-1-944903-08-4

Printed in China

10 9 8 7 6 5 4 3 2 1

Cameron Kids is an imprint of Cameron + Company

Cameron + Company
6 Petaluma Blvd., Suite B6
Petaluma, CA 94952
www.cameronbooks.com

To Zachary and Grace.
I love you more.
Make your mark!
—A.G.

For my Smarties,
Paloma and Mirabel,
and for Uncle Steve, who coaches
with his heart wide open.
—A.K.

Smarty Marty

STEPS UP HER

GAME

CONTENTS

The Greatest Game in the World

"Mitt?"

"Check."

"Cleats?"

"Yep."

"Jersey?"

"Of course I have my jersey—I'm wearing it!" Mikey said.

"Always smart to check," Marty said. "Cap?"

"Oh yeah—forgot my cap."

It was Opening Day of the greatest game in the world. Marty's little brother, Mikey, was playing on the West Side Wingers, their small town's Little League Major Division team. Marty was their official scorekeeper.

While Marty waited for her little brother to grab his cap from his room, she ran through her own checklist: sharpened pencils, eraser, rulebook, scorebook, her lucky cap. Check. Check. Check. Check. Check.

Marty loved baseball. Her nickname around town was "Smarty Marty" because she knew a lot about the game.

Marty had learned how to score from her great-grandmother Martha, whom she was named after. Martha, or Gigi as she was known, had passed away when Marty was younger. She had loved the game, too, and taught Marty everything she knew.

Gigi followed the game faithfully and even kept her own scorebook. Not everyone could play baseball well, but scoring was an even playing field. Gigi could go toe-to-toe with the best of them.

Not everyone expects a girl to be smart about baseball. But Gigi was, and so was Marty.

Marty missed Gigi. She missed having someone to share her love of baseball with.

That's why Marty taught Mikey everything she knew about the game.

Marty would never forget taking her kid brother to his first Big League Baseball game and showing him how to score. Mikey had thought baseball was boring. But since that day, Mikey was hooked. And now Mikey loved listening to scoring stories Marty shared about their great-grandma.

Finally, the two had something in common. Instead of arguing all the time, they actually had real conversations. They would start talking about baseball, but then Mikey would ask Marty about anything . . . school, friends, bugs. Marty was smart about many things.

Best of all, the following spring, Mikey

had decided to take a crack at playing.

Mikey smiled wide beneath his brand-new baseball cap.

Marty tugged on his cap and said, "Let's go, kiddo," and they headed out the door and down the sidewalk to the park.

It was a perfect day for a game.

Marty and Mikey's parents were at the store picking up water and snacks for the team. They'd meet them at the field. Nama would be there, too.

Nama was their grandmother. When Marty was a toddler, she couldn't say, "Grandma." She'd say "Nama" instead—and it stuck. Nama lived just a few miles away and spent a lot of time with them.

"Are you sure you have everything?" Marty asked.

"Marty!"

"I know. I know. I just want to make sure you're ready for your Little League debut," Marty said, winking at him.

"Wait! I knew I was forgetting something." Marty grabbed her lucky baseball from the bottom of her bag.

"Always keep a spare ball inside your glove," she said, tossing the ball to her brother. "It'll break your glove in and make it easier to catch."

Mikey caught the ball in his glove.

"Now I know why they call you Smarty Marty."

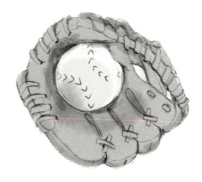

Nine blocks from home, the ball field was buzzing. The two teams were warming up, and fans were starting to fill the bleachers.

Marty spotted their mom and dad and Nama, who waved from the top row on the home team's side. All three were wearing matching ball caps from Mikey's team. In the bleachers, too, were lots of kids from their school, as well as kids from the other schools in town.

Mikey suddenly got quiet, kicking the dirt at his feet. "Uhh . . . Marty, I'm nervous. What if I mess up?"

This was Mikey's very first game, and he wasn't the strongest player on the team. He had just BARELY made it onto the Majors, and most of the kids were bigger than him.

"Everyone gets nervous before a game," Marty said. "It means you're excited. All you can do is your best. And no matter what happens, have fun.

"Now, show your coach you know how to hustle!" Marty pushed Mikey toward the outfield, where the West Side Wingers were stretching in their brand-new orange and black uniforms.

Marty felt like she was giving herself a pep talk, too. She was suddenly feeling a little nervous about scoring the game. What if *she* messed up?

But, as usual, she could hear Gigi's voice saying, "Scoring a game helps keep your head in the game." It was true. As long as she had a pencil in her hand, she wouldn't miss a beat.

Marty had a job to do. She set out for her workstation upstairs in the press box behind home plate. Thoughtfully, she arranged each of her tools on the table in front of her: sharpened pencils, eraser, rulebook, scorebook. She was all set.

Marty had the best seat in the house.

She watched as Mikey and his team fielded grounders and the opposing team—the East Side Eagles—caught pop flies. She couldn't wait to watch Mikey play. How would he do? Would his team win?

That's when she noticed the seat next to hers was empty. The microphone was out, but the game announcer wasn't there yet.

The announcer had the important job of keeping the crowd informed, announcing the batting lineups and explaining important plays. Plus, they got to talk into a microphone, which was pretty cool.

Marty knew how to score a game, but she had never announced one before.

Only minutes away from the first pitch,

both teams ran into their dugouts for quick cheers before the home team took the field.

GO WINGERS!

Marty's stomach flip-flopped. She checked her watch and gulped. The game was about to start! What if the game announcer didn't show up?

Would Marty have to step up her game?

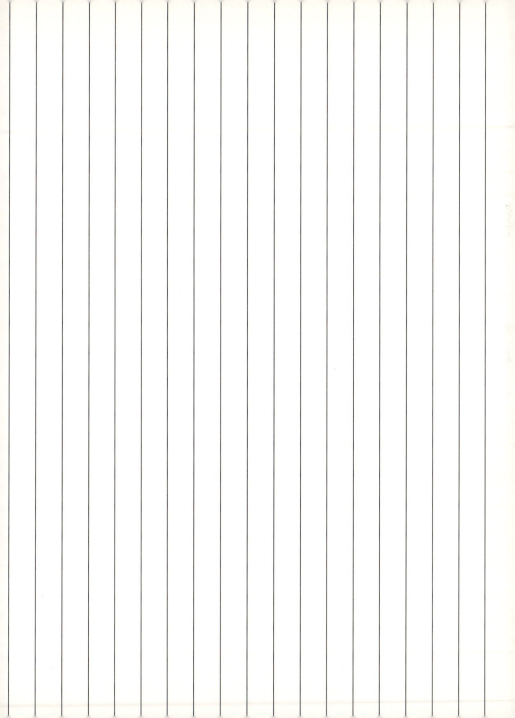

A Whole Other Ball Game

The West Side Wingers rushed from their dugout and spread out across the field. Their pitcher was throwing warm-up pitches to the catcher when Marty saw Mr. Peters walking briskly toward the press box.

Mr. P., as the kids called him, was the

BMOD, or Board Member on Duty, that day for all of the Little League games. He was also her fifth grade teacher.

"Hiya, Marty," Mr. P. said as he ducked inside the press box. "How's our scorekeeping expert today?"

"Doin' well, Mr. P. Excited about my new job this season."

"Funny you should mention that. What do you think about expanding your duties?" Mr. P. asked. "Our announcer won't be able to make it. Do you think you could cover for us this morning?"

Then Mr. P. filled Marty in on the whole story. The league had had one particular boy in mind to announce the games, but he also happened to be a player, and it just wasn't going to work to find a fill-in when he played. They needed someone who could commit to the entire season, and Marty was a perfect fit.

Marty went wide-eyed. All kinds of scenarios started playing out in her mind. What if she mispronounced someone's name? What if she miscalled a play? Everyone would be listening to her. Scoring a game was easy for Marty, but calling a game was a whole other ball game.

"Gee, Mr. P., I don't know. What if I mess up?"

"All you have to do is tell the story of the game," Mr. P. said. "I know you can do that.

I've read your essays."

Nothing ventured is nothing gained. At least that's what Marty's dad always said. Marty was never really sure what it meant, but now she thought she understood. If she didn't try announcing the game, she knew she'd regret it. This was an opportunity that didn't come around often. Everyone wanted to be the announcer. It was one of the most important jobs in baseball.

"I'll do it!" Marty said, raising her chin confidently.

"Thank you, Marty," Mr. P. said, sounding genuinely relieved. He handed her the teams' lineups. "Or, should I say, Smarty Marty?

"Good luck and have fun!"

Mr. P. tipped his hat and was gone, and Marty was all alone. She looked out onto the field. Mikey was playing third base. She knew how he must feel. She felt the same way. But Marty knew from experience that once the first pitch was thrown, the first swing swung, the first out made, everyone could let out a deep breath and just play ball. And score. And announce.

Announce! It was time to announce. The first batter was approaching the plate.

Marty pulled the microphone closer to her and said a tentative "Hello?" into it. Nothing happened. "Is this thing even on?" she mumbled. Fumbling about the microphone stand, she found a switch, and pushed it. A sharp sound reverberated across the field all the way out to the deepest part of the yard. Everyone looked up at the press box. Marty tapped the microphone with her fingers, and the sound of her taps echoed. Yep. The microphone was on.

"Hello!" Marty's voice boomed.

A flock of pigeons pecking about in the outfield took flight.

Marty caught Mikey looking up at the press box window in surprise. She imagined her mom and dad and Nama, sitting in the bleachers below her, equally surprised by the familiar voice of the announcer.

"Welcome to this morning's Majors game, everyone. I'm Marty and I'll be announcing today's contest between the West Side Wingers and the East Side Eagles."

The crowd clapped politely. Marty thought she heard her father whoop.

Mikey had a huge grin on his face. "That's my sister!" he was saying to the left fielder and the shortstop. He gave Marty the thumbs up. Marty winked back.

Marty might never have called a game,

but she'd watched countless ball games on TV with her family. She thought about her favorite announcers and how they'd start each game letting the audience know who was playing which position in the field or the defense. Then they'd move onto the offense and announce the lineup.

How hard could it be? Marty took a deep breath and began.

"On the mound for the West Side Wingers today, Teddy Townsend!

"Playing infield, at first base . . . "

The words began to flow, and Marty took extra pride in calling her brother's position.

"Playing the hot corner, my little brother, Mikey!"

The home crowd cheered. This time Marty DEFINITELY heard her dad whoop. She could also see Mikey trying not to look embarrassed. And then Marty suddenly felt her face flush and realized why: Only his family called him Mikey. Oops.

" . . . Or, Mike, as he likes to be called."

The crowd chuckled.

"Now batting lead-off, Eli Springer."

The crowd for the visiting team cheered, and she could see Mikey getting into "ready position." He kicked the dirt around third base a bit and then gave his glove one good punch. He settled his feet, bent his knees, then dropped his glove and throwing hand to hover just above the dirt.

Teddy was a good pitcher, but Marty knew that if the batters hit the balls, Mikey would be busy, making plays behind Teddy. It wasn't called the hot corner for nothing!

"Go, Mikey!" she shouted, forgetting the mic was on.

The crowd laughed, and now Mikey scowled at her.

Teddy retired the first batter.

"And the pitch . . . Swing and a miss! Strike three, and the East Side Eagles have one out."

Teddy retired the next batter, too.

Then the Eagles' three-hole hitter came up and smacked a single up the middle.

"With two outs and a runner on first,

now up to bat, cleanup hitter, Sammy 'the Smash' Simpson!" Marty announced, adding in Sammy's well-known nickname.

Marty wasn't the only one in town with a nickname. Everyone knew Sammy. He was the best hitter around. He hit home runs . . . A LOT.

Sammy had power, but he wasn't the most consistent hitter. In fact, the previous year Sammy and Marty had both participated in a town-wide "skills" contest that involved hitting and fielding. Marty and Sammy went toe-to-toe on fielding ground balls, but when it came to being able to use the whole field— like hit to left, center, or right—Marty stole the show *and* the medal for best all-around

ball player. Sammy had never quite gotten over it.

The West Side Wingers only needed one out, but Sammy the Smash wouldn't go down easy.

"Here comes the pitch. Fastball on the inside corner is in there for a strike!" Marty called, barely containing her excitement.

Marty could see the shortstop reminding the infield and outfield how many outs the team had and where the outs could be made, and Mikey getting ready.

Teddy got set on the mound and delivered the next pitch.

Sammy the Smash pulled a line drive down the third base line. He hit it so hard Mikey barely had time to react. Luckily it was foul.

"Foul ball!" Marty breathed a sigh of relief.

Two strikes on the Smash.

"Teddy Townsend way ahead in the count with two strikes and no balls. He gets set to deliver . . ."

S M A C K !

The Smash hit a line drive, fair this time, and it was heading straight for Mikey's head!

Sammy the Smash

It appeared Mikey had no time to think as he flung his glove up in "protect" mode, and—SNAP!—the ball hit his glove. Reflex. Pure reflex had saved his face and ended the inning. Mikey had snagged Sammy's smoking line drive right out of the air.

Mikey's teammates high-fived him as they made their way in, and fans of the Wingers jumped up in excitement . . . and relief. Marty took the cue.

"Whoa—that's why they call it the hot corner, folks. A line out to third wraps up the top of the first, no score."

Marty didn't notice the snarl Sammy the Smash Simpson was shooting her way. She also didn't hear him mumble under his breath, "Who put a girl on the mic . . . Seriously?"

Marty put the final touches on her scorecard—a swift diagonal line under Sammy the Smash's box, tallied the runs (0), hits (1), errors (0), and runners left on

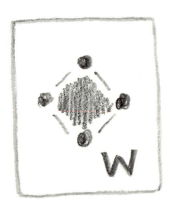

base (1)—and then she turned her attention to the home team's lineup. "Batting lead-off today for the West Side Wingers . . ."

She fell into a familiar rhythm, remembering all of the games she had watched with Gigi. The language of the game rolled off her tongue.

"Base hit up the middle. He hit that one on the screws.

"A one-hopper, this is going to be a tough play to make . . . and the Eagles just get him at first, but the runner advances, and the Wingers have a man in scoring position. One away."

Marty loved moving a runner around on her scorecard. Her pencil took the runner from first to second. "A productive out," she could hear Gigi say.

"A four-pitch walk and now the West Side Wingers have runners on first and second."

Next up to bat: the cleanup hitter. Marty hadn't had time to study the lineups and was taking the names one at a time. She looked at the next name on the list and her voice caught, "uh . . . *ahem* . . . batting cleanup . . . Mike McEntyre," she said, trying not to sound as worried as she felt seeing her little brother at the plate.

Every player in the lineup had an important job, but the cleanup hitter was usually the best hitter on the team. It was a lot of pressure, and Marty's stomach dropped knowing Mikey was responsible for driving in a run.

"The pitcher is set to deliver . . ." Marty began, "it's high. Ball one." But Mikey had swung. It was a strike.

Marty had told him countless times to lay off the high ones. They looked so hittable and fooled most. And now she'd made her first mistake on the mic.

The fans looked back at her. The scoreboard worker, who kept track of balls and strikes, hesitated. The ump threw his hands up in confusion.

"Sorry 'bout that. Strike one," Marty said. She didn't know who she was more annoyed with—her brother or herself.

"The count is oh and one to the batter," *who better not swing at another ball at his head!* Marty thought. She uttered a very quiet "C'mon, Mikey," through gritted teeth.

Marty knew as an announcer you weren't supposed to cheer for or favor a team. It was called being unbiased. But this was different. She had a stake in this at-bat, or AB, as it was known.

Marty thought back to the countless times she threw batting practice to Mikey in their backyard. Pitch after pitch after pitch, discussing the strike zone. Chest high, across the letters. Above the knees. Ya gotta know the zone.

She knew firsthand how hard it was to lay off the high ones. She fell for them often in her own games and hoped Mikey had more discipline at the plate.

The pitcher got set on the mound, began his windup and delivered.

"High and wide for a ball, the count even at one." This time Marty waited until the ump called the pitch.

Mikey went on to work his at-bat to a full

count—three balls, two strikes. One more ball, and he'd walk. One more strike and he'd be out. It was developing into a great AB. Mikey might have been a rookie, but he wasn't going down easy.

The next pitch was on its way . . .

"Foul ball. The count remains full, and this will be the tenth pitch of the at-bat. Runners with their leads, here comes the pitch . . ."

And then everything went into slow motion. Marty saw Mikey lift his left foot and knew this was the pitch. It was right down the pipe. His elbows lifted, his chin dropped, and as the bat came around, she awaited the sweet sound of the crack of the bat. This was it, this was it, he was going to get a hit!

But instead of the aluminum "ting" of a Little League hit, Marty was quickly brought back to real time when she heard the slap of the ball in the catcher's glove.

Boy, baseball was a tough game.

"Strike three," Marty reluctantly called. Mikey was out. The runners stranded. The crowd let out a loud sigh, and Mikey's shoulders slumped as he walked back to his team in the dugout, dragging the bat behind him in the dirt.

Marty had been in Mikey's shoes many times as a player. Even the best players only get a hit three out of ten times.

Gigi's words played through Marty's mind, "Baseball can be cruel. It's a game that will humble you."

Marty wished she could call out, "You'll get 'em next time, Mikey," but all she could do was watch him. She imagined the tears burning his eyes.

Announcing baseball had been Marty's dream, but this wasn't fun. No one had warned her it could be this hard.

Marty looked for her parents in the stands and found her mom, staring back and holding up her hand with their sign for "I love you."

Marty couldn't remember a time they didn't use this silent display of affection. Her mom had taught her and Mikey some

sign language as babies, and the symbol for "I love you" just stuck.

And that's when Marty knew how she could help Mikey. She couldn't TELL him, but she could SHOW him—everything would be okay.

Marty signed "I love you" to Mikey, while he settled in at third. She could see his shoulders relax a bit and knew it had helped.

Sammy the Smash was planning on showing Marty something, too: that baseball was no place for a girl!

Marty Gets the Call

An hour and forty-five minutes after first pitch, the whole family was circled up with a group hug. Despite Mikey's EPIC catch earlier in the game, the team had lost. Mikey striking out and stranding runners didn't help, and he felt bad. His family was trying to cheer him up.

When Marty made her way down from the press box to meet them, the circle of Mom, Dad, Mikey, and Nama opened up to include her, too.

"You were amazing, honey," her mom said. "How in the world did you end up calling the game?"

While briefing her family on how the day's events unfolded, Marty was interrupted by Mr. P.

"Tough loss, Mikey," Mr. P. said, patting him on the head. "But good job on the mic, Marty. Say, would you be interested in announcing more games this season?"

Would she ever!

Marty looked at her parents, who nodded

encouragingly, and then she looked at Mikey, who was giving her a serious stink eye. *What's your problem*? she thought. But she knew the answer. Mikey had just lost his first Little League game, and she was the one getting all the attention. She reached out for Mikey and put her arm around him.

"Mr. P., if it's alright with you, I'd like to talk it over with the star third baseman after we break down his first game."

Mikey's body eased, and he leaned into his big sis. He looked up at her. No words were spoken, but his eyes said thank you.

"That's just fine by me. Give me a call tonight if you're game, and we'll schedule you for next Saturday."

"Marty, we've got to get moving if we're going to make it to *your* game on time," her dad said.

Marty was so wrapped up in announcing her brother's game she totally forgot she had her own game to play. She'd also forgotten her scoring bag in the press box.

"Be right back!" she shouted, running back toward the booth above the field.

Marty was just about to climb the stairs when Sammy the Smash and a few of his teammates stepped in front of her and stopped her cold.

"Smarty Marty, huh?" Sammy said. "More like Farty Marty if you ask me." His teammates snickered.

"Excuse me? What did you say?" Marty said.

"You heard me. Just like we heard you calling the game. We didn't like it and we don't like you. A girl announcer . . ." he said and began to laugh, and then they were all laughing at Marty. "What a joke. *'C'mon, Mikey!'*" Sammy said in a high voice, mimicking Marty. "You don't know anything about baseball."

Marty glared at the Smash, her face turning red with rage.

"As a matter of fact, I do."

Sammy's teammates let out a low *ooooohh*, egging her on. Marty's voice was shaking, but she didn't care. "Tough day at the plate,

huh, Sammy? I know. I scored your game, and you were oh for three. Must be hard when you don't live up to your nickname."

Marty had nailed it. Sammy must have been embarrassed he'd had an "oh for" day at the plate, and, in front of a girl. His teammates were now laughing at him.

"You don't know squat. You can't even tell a ball from a strike. Girls suck, and you stink as an announcer. Everyone was laughing at how bad you were. Stick to softball."

Marty's eyes burned with tears.

"Oh look, now she's gonna cry. I told you girls weren't cut out for baseball. What a baby. Are they letting babies call games now, Marty? No wonder you got the job!

You might want to think long and hard about Mr. P.'s offer to call another game," Sammy threatened, and then he clipped her shoulder as he pushed past her.

Marty stared straight ahead, shocked. One of the best days of her life had just turned into one of the worst.

Did Sammy really think a girl couldn't call a game as well as a boy? Did everyone think this? Were they really laughing at her during the game?

She felt like someone had knocked the wind out of her, and it hurt . . . a lot.

"Marty, c'mon. We're gonna be late for your game," she heard her dad call near the parking lot.

Tears fell down her face. How in the world was she going to go play a softball game knowing the whole town thought she was a joke? She closed her eyes tight to try and stop the tears. She thought of Gigi. She knew just what she would say: "Don't you dare let Sammy the Smash bring you down. You're better than that. He's picking on you because he's embarrassed by how he played. Stop your crying and hold your chin up."

Marty was sure when she opened her eyes, Gigi would be right there in front of her. Her words were so clear. But when she opened her eyes, Mikey was standing there looking at her with concern.

"Why are you crying, Marty?"

Marty wiped the tears away fiercely. "Allergy attack, phew, bad one."

She ran upstairs and grabbed her scoring bag. Something slipped out and fell to the ground. Marty bent down to pick it up. It was a picture of her and Gigi that she kept as a memento in her rulebook. Gigi was always with her.

On the way out she said, "C'mon, Mikey, I've got a game to play and a call to make to Mr. P. I'm taking the announcing job."

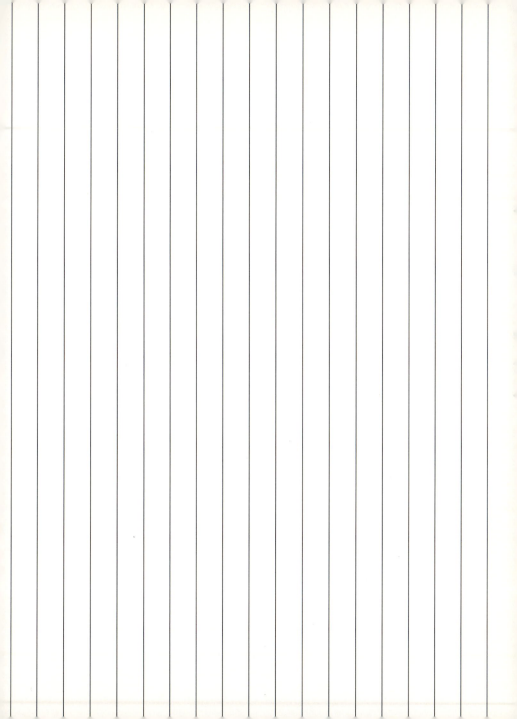

A Girl in a Boy's World

Marty arrived at her game in the nick of time. Her coach, while AWESOME, was very strict. He had team rules and the number one rule: BE ON TIME.

Marty hustled over to the dugout, hung up her equipment bag, grabbed her glove, and quickly found her best friend, Rue.

She felt so lucky she and Rue were drafted on the same team. They had been friends since kindergarten, and playing ball together only made them closer. Rue threw the ball to Marty, and they fell into

the rhythm of playing catch.
But Marty was distracted,
and Rue could tell.

"How was your
brother's game?" she
asked, winding up
to throw.

W H O M P H.
The ball landed
squarely in Marty's
glove.

"You're never
gonna believe
what happened . . ."

W H O M P H.
She threw the ball
hard back to Rue.

Marty recapped the morning's events while Rue listened intently, the two tossing the ball perfectly between them through the entire story.

"Marty, you know what? You rock. I don't know anyone brave enough to stand up to Sammy the Smash."

"Yeah, but what about at school? I've got a target on my back now. He thinks girls don't know anything about baseball, and he's gonna tell the whole school that I was awful."

"Anyone who knows you won't believe him. You're Smarty Marty, for crying out loud," Rue said. "He's just mad because he played badly in front of you. He doesn't even know that you could care less. You just like the game, no matter how someone plays. Maybe you should just talk to him and see what his problem is."

Rue's face turned coy as she added, "He probably has a crush on you!"

Marty turned red. "Ewww!" The thought made the girls laugh hysterically.

Marty turned serious again, the encounter with Sammy weighing heavily on her heart. "His problem is me and the fact that I'm a girl in a BOY'S world. A girl who can talk ball is not welcome. He made that crystal clear."

"Nothing you can do about that, Marty. You can't change who you are. And you shouldn't. Not for anyone or anything."

Marty took her usual position at first base. Rue's words lingered in her mind. Her friend played close by at second. Between innings the two girls were joined at the hip, talking and plotting out various plans

of action should Sammy make good on his threat.

Before Marty knew it, the third baseman, the shortstop, and the entire outfield were all in on the conversation and offering advice on how to silence Sammy.

Marty loved the camaraderie of her team. They trusted each other, they could confide in one other and the friendships continued beyond the diamond. She loved her friends.

Her coach, however, wasn't thrilled with all of the excessive chatter and chimed in himself, "Ladies . . . where's the focus today? Are your minds on the game, 'cause it doesn't sound like it!"

Marty and her teammates shot to attention knowing their coach always meant business. They all looked at one another and smiled. They knew the Sammy saga was far from over and they'd get back to it right after they "took it" to the other team.

Sure enough, Marty's team got the "W."

While sitting in the dugout afterward, her teammates convinced Marty that it was a risk to stand up to Sammy, but reminded her that "you can't steal second base without taking your foot off first."

Taking the announcing gig was the only way to go. Sure, Sammy would try and embarrass her at school and at the next game she called. But the only way he would eventually stop was if Marty found a way to outlast him. And what was the worst that could happen? Would he stick a sign on her back? Put something gross in her locker?

Marty could handle whatever he threw at her.

She had thick skin. It was the other thing

she had inherited from Gigi, besides her love of baseball. She'd gotten used to people giving her the "double-take"—a girl keeping score at the boys' baseball game. Usually they smiled and gave her a thumbs up.

Loving baseball and knowing the game was never something she had had to defend before. No one had ever made her feel like she didn't belong. So why did Sammy? There had to be more to this than Sammy just being mean.

Marty wondered if he might still be sore because she was named best all-around ball player in town. Or was there more?

What was most disappointing for Marty was that she had actually respected how good of a player Sammy was. She had been looking forward to scoring his games and wished she could be excited about calling them.

Marty and her teammates were packing up their bags when she saw Sammy walking by with his crew. They slowed down to a daunting pace as they passed by the dugout. Sammy spotted her and taunted, "See you at school on Monday, Marty."

Marty froze. Sammy smirked. In an instant, Rue was by her side. Then her whole squad was standing behind her, arms crossed, glaring right back at the Smash. Gigi, too. Marty could hear her say, "Stand your ground, Marty." And she stood a little bit taller.

"Looking forward to it, Sammy," Marty said confidently, but Marty KNEW she wouldn't get any sleep until after her school day was over on Monday.

Little did she know that Sammy didn't have plans to make her life miserable at school. Oh no. But her little brother, Mikey? Now that was a different story.

Outsmarted

Monday arrived, and with it, heavy dread. Marty had tossed and turned all night. She was so tired, but her mind wouldn't stop imagining all of the ways in which Sammy might try to embarrass her.

"You feel okay, Marty?" her mom asked at

breakfast. She put the back of her hand on Marty's forehead, feeling for a fever.

"I'm fine," Marty said. But the truth was, she had no appetite. She flipped her cereal over her spoon, watching it drop back into the bowl.

"You've barely eaten any breakfast."

"I'm fine, Mom," Marty snapped.

"Alright, alright," her mom said, throwing both hands up defensively. "Just doing my job as your MOTHER to make sure you're okay." And she went back to getting her things together for her work day.

Marty's dad chimed in from the kitchen island where he was making lunches for the family. "You know, honey, if you need to talk about anything . . ."

"I know, I know," Marty cut him off, "I can tell you and Mom anything and you promise to listen, yadda yadda yadda. I got it, Dad."

Marty's parents stole wide-eyed glances at each other, and Mikey looked back and forth between his mom and his sister and his sister and his dad. This seemed to be happening more often these days.

Marty wasn't ready to tell her mom and dad what was going on with Sammy, but she would catch Mikey up on it during the bus ride home. She couldn't keep any secrets from him. He knew her too well.

"You two ready?" their mom said, slinging her tote bag over her shoulder and leaning in to give their dad a kiss goodbye. "Teeth brushed, shoes on, sweatshirts, backpacks, lunches. Let's go, let's go, let's go! Don't want to be late."

Marty was jumpy when she got to school. Rue tapped her on her shoulder from behind, and Marty nearly flew out of her shoes.

"Hey, sorry," Rue said. "Didn't mean to scare you. Have you seen Sammy yet?"

"No. I didn't sleep last night, and I feel like I'm gonna throw up."

"You'll be okay," Rue said.

They made it to their classroom safe and sound. No sign of the Smash. *Could he be home sick?* Marty wondered. No such luck. Just then she saw him walk by her classroom window on the way to his room next door. Marty braced herself. Chin high. But Sammy didn't even look over. Maybe he had changed his mind. Maybe he forgot.

The morning was uneventful. Marty knew Sammy couldn't do anything to her while they were in class. But when the bell rang for lunch, her stomach started turning again. Anything could happen on the playground. *Oh boy, here we go*, she thought.

Marty, Rue, and the softball crew grabbed their usual table in the cafeteria. Marty tried to look around nonchalantly, but one of her teammates called her out.

"You can relax, Marty. Sammy's not here."

She couldn't help but smile. Her teammates really were looking out for her.

She opened her lunch box and as usual there was a note from her mom. Every day Marty's mom packed her an inspirational message and, nine times out of ten, it was about baseball. Today's note read, "Good players inspire themselves. Great players inspire others." And then she added, "You inspire me, Marty. Have a great day."

Digging into their sandwiches and snacks, Marty's teammates schemed and chatted about what the Smash might try and pull, and by the end of the lunch period, Marty felt they had covered all the bases.

Heading back to her class, Rue pointed, "There he is, Marty."

Marty looked toward the playground. She could only see Sammy's back bookended by a few of his friends. "What's he doing over there?" she wondered aloud.

Then, as if Sammy had heard her, he and his brood turned toward Marty, and there was her terrified little brother standing behind them. He looked so small! Sammy made a fist with his right hand and punched the open palm of his left.

Suddenly it clicked. Sammy and his crew weren't going to make life miserable for Marty. They were going to make life miserable for Mikey. A chill went up Marty's spine, and she felt her stomach drop.

Sammy started to walk toward Marty, and Mikey fled to his classroom.

"Oh hey, Marty," Sammy said in passing,

"if you can't take a hint, maybe your little brother can."

"That's your big plan, Sammy? To go after my little brother? No wonder they call you the Smash. You're not a baseball star. You're just a bully," Marty said, enraged. Her teammates gathered around her and tried to calm her down.

Sammy stopped in his tracks and turned back toward Marty.

"Baseball. Is. For. Boys! Remember that, Marty. No one wants a girl behind the mic. You can't do the job." Sammy slammed past, and this time Marty almost fell to the ground.

Had Sammy outsmarted her?

Marty never thought he'd go after her little brother. But now it made sense. This was an all-new low. She felt horrible. Was Mikey okay? She'd have to wait until the bus ride home to find out.

One thing was for sure. There was no way she could take the announcing job now. Not if it put her brother in danger. She'd tell Mikey first thing after school. She wouldn't take the job. Sammy had won this game.

Batting Cleanup

The final moments of class took forever.

TICK.

TICK.

TICK.

Marty stared at the clock. Her right foot nervously tapped under her desk.

"Everything alright, Marty?" Mr. P. asked. "Looks like you're having a little trouble sitting still."

Marty didn't even hear Mr. P. calling her name. She was locked in on the clock.

"Marty . . . *ahem,* MARTY!" Rue nudged her from the neighboring desk. "Mr. P. asked you a question."

"What? Oh yeah. All good, Mr. P. ALL GOOD."

But Marty was anything but good. She couldn't shake what had happened at lunch, Sammy the Smash picking on her little brother. She felt sick to her stomach wondering what he had said to Mikey. What she knew for sure was that Sammy had scared him and that made her want to SMASH the Smash!

When the bell finally rang, Marty sprang out of her seat and raced for the bus where she found Mikey sitting in the back, his eyes red. No one else would notice, but Marty was his sister and she knew. It was official. Sammy the Smash had made her brother cry.

"Mikey," she said, slipping into the seat in front of him, her back facing the driver.

"Are you o—"

"DO NOT SPEAK TO ME," Mikey said through gritted teeth. He turned to look out the window.

This was even worse than Marty thought. Whatever Sammy said had not only made Mikey scared, but also mad at her.

"Mikey, what did Sammy say?"

"Just leave me alone, Marty."

Marty knew better than to poke an angry tiger. She turned around and sat in silence the rest of the ride home.

When they got to their bus stop, Mikey blew past her in the aisle and walked several feet ahead of her all the way home. Usually they walked together and talked about their

day. Or they talked about baseball. This walk home was breaking Marty's heart. Mikey wouldn't talk to her. He wouldn't even look at her.

Their mom was in the kitchen, waiting for their usual afternoon hellos and school-day recaps. Things were different today.

"Hi guys," she said.

Mikey went straight to his room and slammed the door.

"What in the world is going on with your brother?" Marty's mom asked.

"Just let me . . . ugh, I gotta go talk to him, Mom. I'll fill you in, but I gotta try and fix this."

Marty's mom must have seen the urgency

and concern on Marty's face. "Go. Go fix it. Whatever it is that needs fixing."

Marty sprinted upstairs to Mikey's room on her mom's first "go." She could still hear her mom talking to herself. She did that sometimes.

Marty quietly knocked on Mikey's door. A hand-written sign read KEEP OUT.

"Mikey, I know you're mad at me. Please let me come in and talk to you."

"Go. Away."

"Mikey, please."

"There's nothing to say. Sammy the Smash is going to beat me up and pour slushies over my head if you don't quit the announcing job."

Marty nudged the door open and found Mikey sitting on the floor, arms crossed, staring at the ground, his collection of baseball cards scattered around him.

"Is that what Sammy said to you at lunch today? That he was going to beat you up?" Marty crept in and sat on the carpet across from him. Mikey's anger had settled a bit.

"He said a lot of mean things, but yeah, that pretty much covers it. 'Your sister is hanging out where she doesn't belong. Your sister is gonna get you hurt. What color is your favorite slushie to wear?'"

"Mikey, I'm so sorry. I never thought Sammy would come after you. I was expecting him to come after me. You know he threatened me, too, at the park this past weekend."

"Is that why you were crying?"

So Mikey hadn't believed her when she said she had allergies. He did know her well.

"Why is it so important to you?" Mikey asked.

"What?"

"Baseball. Why do you need everyone to know how smart you are about baseball?" Mikey was now half-heartedly shuffling through his collection of baseball cards. "It's kind of embarrassing."

Embarrassing? Wow, Marty hadn't seen that coming. She took a second to respond.

"I guess I never really thought that

because I was a girl I couldn't love baseball. Gigi would tell me stories about people staring at her because she was scoring a game and not playing with dolls. She never wanted me to feel that way, like I didn't belong.

"Gigi loved baseball, and I love baseball because it's a game that makes you think . . . no matter who you are. And even if you don't play, you can appreciate it, boy or girl. I love baseball for so many reasons, but the biggest is it reminds me of Gigi. It makes me feel close to her.

"Do you know what I love more than baseball?" Marty asked.

Mikey shrugged.

"You."

Mikey stuck his tongue out and rolled his eyes back as if he were gagging, but Marty saw that he was blushing a bit, too.

"I'll call Mr. P. tonight and let him know I won't be taking the announcing job."

Marty thought this announcement would make Mikey happy, but he didn't even look up from his baseball cards.

Just then the phone rang. Marty heard movement outside Mikey's door. Had their mom been standing outside the door the whole time? Had she heard everything?

"Hello?" she heard her mom answer the phone downstairs, slightly out of breath. "Oh, hello, Mrs. Sterling."

It was the school principal. Marty and Mikey looked at each other wide-eyed. Why would the principal be calling their house? Was Marty in trouble?

A Good Call

Marty's mom got off the phone and turned around to find both of her children staring at her, anxious to know why the principal had called their home.

"Heyyyy—a little space, huh?" Marty's mom joked.

"Why did Mrs. Sterling call, Mom?" Mikey blurted out. Marty could tell he was worried Sammy would make good on his threats if he thought Mikey had tattled.

"Why don't you let me worry about that for now. Marty, I would like to have a word with you. But I'm going to speak with Mikey first about what I hear was an eventful day. Wait for me in your room, okay?"

Marty went to her room and sprawled out on her bed with a huge sigh. Why was this happening? She was dreading making the phone call to Mr. P. She'd never quit anything before, and her stomach started to feel queasy thinking about it.

While she waited for her mom, she stared

at the ceiling and played out different ways she could tell Mr. P. she was going to quit.

"I just don't think it's gonna work out . . .

"My Saturdays are just so busy . . .

"Maybe I should just concentrate on scoring . . ."

And then she heard her mom's knock on the door. "Marty? Can I come in?"

"Sure, come in, Mom."

"How's my favorite girl?" her mom asked, sitting on the bed.

"I'm your only girl," Marty said, rolling her eyes. Her mom always said that.

Marty had been putting on a brave face since Sammy pulled his stunt at the ballpark last weekend. But today, watching her brother get picked on was just too much, and she couldn't keep it in. She buried her face in her hands, and the tears began to flow. Her mother hugged her.

"Marty, honey, what's the matter? What sparked the waterworks?"

"Oh, Mom, I don't know what to do. I don't know how to fix it."

"Why don't you start by telling me what happened and let's see if I can help."

Marty spilled it. She told her mom everything. From Sammy the Smash threatening her at the ballpark, to showing up at her game, to the awful scene at school.

Marty's mom listened intently, nodded her head, and murmured "mmm hmm" a lot.

When Marty was done talking, her mom took a deep breath and, while gently pulling stray hairs back from Marty's face, calmly said, "Marty, this is only the first of so many tests for you. You are a girl trying to be part of the 'boy' world of baseball."

"But mom, it's not—"

"Ah, ah—let me finish . . . You don't know this yet, so I'm going to let you in on a secret. YOU . . . are an inspiration, a trailblazer, a leader. You have the opportunity to be the first girl announcer in our town's Little League, and no one, especially Sammy the Smash, can stop you . . . unless you let him.

"Anything worth having in life won't come easy. You have to fight for it. And sometimes you have to fight extra hard when you're a girl. If you quit now, you'll always regret it. Believe me on this.

"There's a little girl out there, much smaller than you who will see you calling a baseball game and not even think twice about whether or not she should be there, because she saw you there. Being an inspiration and a role model isn't easy. But it's necessary for those who CAN, to DO!"

Then Marty's mom began to rub her back. It always helped settle her down.

"I know how upsetting it was to see Sammy target your brother. We had a long talk, and I have a very good feeling that it will all work out. Your father and I will make sure

Mikey is safe. And it's also our job to make sure you're okay. If you decide you want to quit the announcing job because YOU don't think it's the right fit, we will support your decision. But if you're quitting because of Sammy the Smash, I strongly urge you to reconsider."

Just then, Marty heard another knock on the door and turned to see Mikey.

"Marty, you're really good at it . . . the announcing thing. You love baseball more than anything. I can handle whatever Sammy's gonna pull, as long as you are doing what you love."

"I'm scared," Marty said, looking down. "I'm afraid, and I'm so mad that I'm afraid."

"Oh, honey—it's okay to be afraid," Marty's mom said. "But what is it exactly you're afraid of?"

Marty was still looking down, until her mom cupped her chin and gently pulled her head up so their eyes met. Marty's eyes welled up with tears. Her lip quivered.

"What if Sammy's right? I'm afraid I'm not good enough and I don't belong."

Marty's mom's eyes began to well up with tears now, too.

"I remember how hard it is to be eleven years old and question EVERYTHING. If only I knew then what I know now." Marty's mom suddenly looked wistful.

"My heart aches for you, Marty, but I also

know that you are the best young baseball announcer in town. And do you know what Gigi told me a long time ago?"

"No," Marty choked, tears streaming down her face.

"She said, 'The only way someone can make you feel bad about yourself is if YOU LET THEM.' Do you understand?"

Marty was confused. She shook her head.

Her mom continued, "Don't give Sammy the power or satisfaction of making you feel bad. Don't quit, Marty. Stick it out. Like Mikey said, you are very good at what you do.

"And I'm here. Your dad and Mikey are here with you. And you know Gigi is looking down on you—always. We love you.

"What do you say we all go out and grab an ice cream?"

Marty's mom always knew the right things to say and do. Ice cream was always a good call.

Marty

Mikey

But after enjoying a treat with her family, the anxiety started to set in again. Especially when Marty glanced at the game schedule on the fridge.

"Are you kidding me?" Marty said to herself, banging her head against the fridge. Mikey's team was to face Sammy's team again on Saturday. Another encounter with Sammy was inevitable.

Marty thought back to the phone call her mom received from Mrs. Sterling. There was more to that conversation than her mom was letting on.

Game Day

Saturday. Game day.

Usually it was Marty's favorite day of the week. She would jump out of bed. Throw her hair in a pony, don her lucky ball cap, and get ready for a day at the yard. But this Saturday felt more like Doomsday.

Sammy had kept his distance all week, but what he didn't know was that Marty had decided to continue with the announcing job. She dreaded what Sammy would say. Or worse, what Sammy was going to do.

"Marty," her mom called. "Breakfast is ready. Hustle up. You're going to be late."

Marty dragged herself out of bed and walked down the stairs as slow as molasses. Mikey was already at the table devouring his breakfast. She couldn't believe it. He looked like he didn't have a care in the world.

"Hey, Marty," Mikey said. "Whoa!—You gonna brush your hair?"

Yep. Clearly Mikey felt perfectly fine! He was dressed in his baseball uniform and already teasing her. Just a normal Saturday for him. Oh, to be nine again!

Marty's mom placed a plate of hot chocolate-chip pancakes in front of her. It was her favorite breakfast, but she had no appetite this morning. Her mom put her arms around her and whispered in her ear, "Everything will be alright. You've got this."

Marty took a deep breath and nodded her head. Her mom had never steered her wrong. She was glad her parents had convinced her to stick with the announcing gig. No matter what Sammy the Smash threatened to do, she needed to prove to him she was not going to back down.

A girl DID belong at the ballpark and a

girl COULD call a game . . . just as well as any boy.

While Marty waited for her little brother, she ran through her checklist: sharpened pencils, eraser, rulebook, scorebook, her lucky cap. Check. Check. Check. Check. Check.

The nine-block walk to the park seemed like a marathon. Mikey had a little skip in his step and Marty was really annoyed.

"Why are you so chipper?" she asked.

"It's Saturday. It's baseball. Why are you such a Debby Downer?" he replied.

"Uhhhh, in case you forgot, I'm about to be humiliated by the meanest boy in school!"

"Marty—Mom said everything would be

alright. You gotta trust her and you gotta trust yourself. You're gonna have a great day. I can feel it!"

She didn't feel it. She just felt sick.

FINALLY, they got to the park. The familiar sounds soothed Marty a bit—the constant chatter, the ting of the ball hitting the bat, the snap of a ball hitting a glove. Lots of people were milling around, but no sign of Sammy . . . yet.

Mikey sprinted to his team, who had just started to warm up and play catch. Marty made her way to the press box, where she unpacked her bag and started to get things in order.

The coaches brought Marty their lineups,

and her stomach sank a little bit more when she saw that Sammy the Smash was batting cleanup against Mikey's team.

It was time for the welcoming remarks. Marty plugged in the mic, and it made a loud screeching noise that echoed around the field.

"Uh . . . sorry, um . . . good morning, everyone. Welcome to Fullerton Little League Field. Today's ten a.m. contest will be between the East Side Eagles and the West Side Wingers. First pitch is about fifteen minutes away, so please visit the snack shack for some goodies before the game begins."

Not too bad, thought Marty. And then she

saw him. Sammy was in the dugout and he wasn't alone. He was talking with his coach and the school principal. What in the world was Mrs. Sterling doing there? Did this have something to do with the phone call her mother had received?

She quickly looked to the stands where her parents were sitting and made eye contact with her mother. Her mom put her fingers in the sign of a "V" and pointed them at her own eyes and then pointed them toward Marty. It was their sign that meant "I see you" and "Everything will be okay."

Marty saw Sammy slump down onto the bench. Was he crying? Mrs. Sterling left the dugout and headed to the stands, while

Sammy's coach headed straight for the press box. Straight for Marty.

"Got a lineup change for the game, Marty," Sammy's coach said.

"Uh, okay Coach . . . I'm ready."

"Sammy has been scratched. He won't be playing today. And for the record, he won't play for me again if he pulls another stunt like he did with you and your brother. Being a bully is not tolerated in baseball, no matter how good you are. Hey . . . have a good call, okay?"

Marty couldn't believe it. She thought Sammy the Smash could get away with anything. Or at least that's how he acted. But she had stuck it out. And now Sammy was sitting in the bleachers, his head in his hands. She couldn't help it, but she actually felt a little sorry for him.

Marty was sure she'd find out more to the story, but right now she had a game to call.

Marty had the best day behind the microphone, and Mikey had a great day at the plate. She called double plays, a couple of home runs, a caught stealing, even a squeeze play. The game was jam-packed with action, and she was loving every minute.

There were still three outs to go. The Smash's team had the lead heading into the bottom of the sixth, and Mikey's team was trying to make the most of it. With the bases loaded, Mikey's team was down by 3 and

Mikey was up to bat. Baseball just didn't get any better than this.

"Bases loaded. Winning run at the plate. Here comes the pitch . . . fastball down the middle and Mikey gets ahold of it. He hits it high, he hits it deep, and . . . It. Is. Outta here! A walk-off grand slam for the West Side Wingers, who win it 7-6! Can you believe it? What a game. The team is celebrating its come-from-behind victory at home plate, and this one, folks, may be in the books, but will be talked about for many days to come. Catch you next Saturday for more Fullerton Little League action. I'm Smarty Marty, and I'll see ya next time."

YES!!! That, Marty thought, *was amazing.*

Her little brother was the hero. She had just had the best call EVER, and she had "smashed" Sammy the Smash. She was so glad she had listened to her parents and didn't quit. She was on cloud nine as fans and players crowded around her and told her what a great job she had done.

"Great call, Marty!"

"You go, girl!"

"Can't wait to hear you next week!"

She was attempting to navigate through the crowd when her parents and Mikey appeared on one side and Sammy the Smash appeared on the other.

Sammy's mom was behind him and gave him a forceful nudge.

"Uh . . . Marty? Mikey? I need to apologize to you both. I'm sorry I was so mean. Mikey, I was wrong to push you around. It won't happen again. Marty . . . I was really mad you got the announcing job. I was supposed to get it, but Mr. P. told me it wasn't going to work out because of my game schedule. When I found out YOU got it and YOU beat me last year for best all-around player, I kind of lost it . . . I was . . . "

Another nudge from his mom.

"I am . . . jealous. But, I had a chance to REALLY listen to you since I didn't get to play today, and, well . . . you're REALLY good. You know the game, and I was wrong to say that because you're a girl you wouldn't know baseball as well as a boy. You proved me wrong and, well, I'm sorry."

It all made sense now. Sammy had been upset with her for a long time, and he was hurt he didn't get the job. But in the end, he loved the game as much as Marty.

Marty was very proud at that moment, and she knew Gigi was looking down on her smiling. She stood her ground, and just like her mom said, everything was okay. And maybe there was even a chance she and Sammy could be friends. Maybe.

"Thanks, Sammy. You're a really good baseball player, and I look forward to calling more of your games."

Marty held her head high and her hand

out to Sammy. He took it. They shook.

Marty and her family headed home, arm in arm in arm in arm, leaving Fullerton Field in the distance . . . until next Saturday!

Smarty Marty

AMY G

How old were you when you were introduced to baseball?
My earliest baseball memory is from when I was four years old.

Do you remember the very first baseball game you went to?
I don't remember my first game. I just remember ALWAYS being at the ballpark in my hometown. I also have many memories of going to A's and Giants games as a kid.

Who is your favorite baseball player?
My favorite baseball player growing up was Dave Stewart. I loved Rickey Henderson, too, and really liked Will Clark.

Where did you grow up?
I grew up in Petaluma, California, where I live today.

Who was your best friend?
My best childhood friend was Carey. She played softball with me.

When you were my age, what did you want to be when you grew up?

When I was your age, I didn't think much about what I wanted to be when I grew up. Life was so busy with ball games. But I did play pretend news anchor, so I must have had some idea TV was in my future.

When did you know you wanted to be a reporter?

In college I did several internships and felt fairly confident I would pursue a career in television. The reporter part developed later. My first job in TV was as a producer.

How did you become an in-game reporter?

Several years of producing features and pre/post-game shows put me in the right place at the right time when a position opened up.

What is a challenge that you face in your work?

Being taken seriously.

Any advice for a girl who wants to become a sports reporter or announcer?

Prepare and KNOW the sport you cover. The margin for error in the male-dominated industry of sports is slim for women. Don't give them something to criticize you for that you should know. And grow a VERY thick skin.

What is your favorite thing about your job?

Getting to interact with Giants fans, especially girl Giants fans who love baseball as much as I do!

Who is a mentor or an inspiration to you?

My children serve as an inspiration to be a good person every day. My husband, Paul, a sports journalist, has been a mentor and sounding board my entire career.

What do you do in the off-season?

Write books! I spend time with my children, host/ emcee events, and run my own social media business.

Favorite quote you live by?

"It ain't about how hard you hit, it's how hard you can get hit and keep moving forward. That's how winning is done."—Rocky Balboa

Favorite color?

Green.

Favorite ice cream flavor?

Peanut butter and chocolate!

AMY GUTIERREZ

is the San Francisco Giants in-game reporter for Comcast SportsNet Bay Area. Raised in Petaluma, California, Amy G, as she is known, spent her childhood watching or playing sports. She learned to score baseball from her mom, to play baseball from her dad, and to love baseball from her grandmother. She is the author of *Smarty Marty's Got Game*, illustrated by Adam McCauley, and *Smarty Marty's Official Gameday Scorebook*.

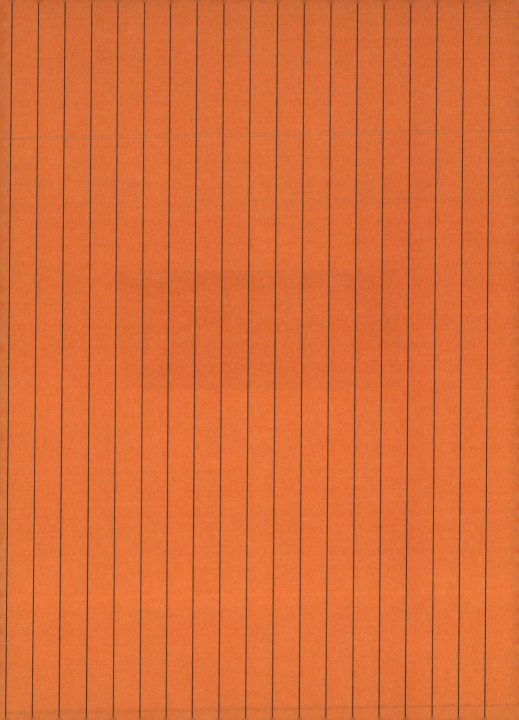